Puppy Friends #1

Gus the Greedy Puppy

by Jenny Dale

Illustrated by Frank Rodgers

Aladdin Paperbacks

Look for these Puppy Friends books!

#1 Gus the Greedy Puppy
#2 Lily the Lost Puppy

Coming soon

#3 Spot the Sporty Puppy
#4 Lenny the Lazy Puppy

First Aladdin Paperbacks edition January 2000

Text copyright © 1999 by Working Partners Limited
Illustrations copyright © 1999 by Frank Rodgers
Activity Fun Pages text copyright © 2000 by Stasia Ward Kehoe
First published by Macmillan Children's Books U.K.
Created by Working Partners Limited

Aladdin Paperbacks
An imprint of Simon & Schuster
Children's Publishing Division
1230 Avenue of the Americas
New York, NY 10020

The text for this book was set in Palatino.
Printed and bound in the United States of America
2 4 6 8 10 9 7 5 3 1

Library of Congress Catalog Card Number: 99-67697
ISBN 0-689-83423-3

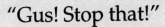

Chapter One

"Gus! Stop that!"

Gus didn't stop. He was enjoying himself. He'd found one of Mr. Carter's ties lying on the bedrooom floor and he was chewing it to bits.

"Gus!" Holly shouted again as she ran up the stairs toward him. "Give me that!"

No way! Gus thought. He hung on to one end of the tattered tie as Holly grabbed the other, and they both began to pull.

"Let go, Gus!" Holly squealed. "Dad's going to be mad when he sees what you've done!"

Gus couldn't understand why. After all, Holly's dad only put the tie around his neck. It didn't *do* anything. Gus could have much more fun with it!

"Gus!"

At the sound of Mrs. Carter's stern voice behind him, Gus suddenly decided that he'd had enough fun with Mr. Carter's tie after all. He let go, and Holly fell backward, landing on her bottom.

"Oh no! And it's his favorite tie!" Mrs. Carter stared sternly at the puppy. "You're a very naughty boy, Gus!"

Gus decided it was time for his best "I'm sorry" look. He slumped down and put his head on his paws. His big brown eyes looked up sadly at Mrs. Carter and Holly.

"Oh, isn't he sweet?" Holly kneeled down and cuddled him. Gus wagged his tail joyfully and rolled over to let her tickle his fat little tummy.

"He's a monster," Mrs. Carter said, but she was trying not to smile. "Here, Holly, you'd better go and put this in the trash can. And let's hope your dad doesn't notice it's gone. He still hasn't realized his leather gloves have disappeared, too."

Gus wondered if they'd found Mr. Carter's slippers—the ones he'd hidden behind the sofa to chew on a little when he was bored. He hoped not. He'd hardly started on the left one yet.

Holly went downstairs with the

remains of the tie, and Gus raced after her. He was hungry, and he was sure it was time for his next meal. He bounced into the kitchen and sat down hopefully by his empty bowl.

"Oh, Gus!" sighed Mrs. Carter as she followed them in. "You can't be hungry again." She looked at the clock. "You had your lunch only half an hour ago!"

Gus couldn't understand what the round thing on the wall was. Or what it had to do with whether he was fed or not. He glared up at it, wishing he could reach it—he'd chew it to pieces.

"Here, Gus," Holly whispered, slipping him a dog biscuit while her mother was busy at the sink. Gus wolfed it down gratefully and gave her a big lick on the nose. Holly giggled and hugged him.

"That dog could win a gold medal for eating!" Mrs. Carter shook her head as she turned on the water. "And what he doesn't eat, he chews!"

But I'm hungry, Gus thought grumpily. He barked a few times, but Mrs. Carter shook her head.

"No, Gus. You've had quite enough."

"No, I haven't," Gus woofed to himself. He waited until Mrs. Carter and Holly were busy doing the dishes, then he trotted out of the kitchen door into the backyard.

It was a warm, sunny day, but Gus didn't even stop to chase the butterflies.

He hurried over to the fence and wriggled through a small gap into Mr. Smith's backyard.

Mr. Smith was sitting in a deck chair with a plate of cheese sandwiches on his knee. Gus was delighted. He loved cheese sandwiches. He bounded over to Mr. Smith, barking a greeting.

"Hello, Gus." The old man put down his newspaper and patted the puppy on the head. "How did you know I was having my lunch? You always arrive at just the right moment!"

Gus shared Mr. Smith's plate of cheese sandwiches, then said goodbye and went next door to the Burtons' house.

Emma, who was in Holly's class at school, was playing in the yard with her little brother, Paul. Jock, their Westie terrier, was there too. Emma and Paul were eating sour cream and chive potato chips. Gus's favorite flavor was barbeque, but he liked sour cream and chive too, so he hurried over to them.

"Oh no, not you again!" Jock barked as Emma and Paul made a big fuss of Gus. "Doesn't Holly feed you?"

"Of course she does!" Gus growled as he crunched up all the chips the children were giving him. "But I'm still hungry!"

Gus stayed until all the chips were finished, then moved on. Mr. Graham, who lived at Number 7, wasn't at home, but Gus got some chicken from Mrs. Patel at Number 9 and a rice cake from the Mortons' baby at Number 11.

By now, Gus was beginning to feel quite full. He decided it was time to go home. There was only one house left on the street anyway, and it wasn't on Gus's usual route. Mrs. Wilson, who lived at

Number 13, didn't like dogs. Instead she had a snooty white Persian cat called Lulu, who walked up and down the street with her nose in the air.

Gus was about to head for home when he smelled something. He stopped in his tracks and sniffed. He sniffed again. It was a delicious smell, warm and fruity and spicy. And it was coming from Mrs. Wilson's house.

Gus had to find out what it was. He hurried back across the Mortons' lawn to look for another gap he'd noticed in the fence. This one led into Mrs. Wilson's garden.

It was a rather tight squeeze, but Gus managed to push his way through. The kitchen door stood open, and the smell was getting stronger and more delicious by the minute.

Gus creeped up to the doorway and peered inside. He didn't want to meet Mrs. Wilson or Lulu. But the kitchen was empty.

Something was bubbling in a big pan on top of the stove. On a big wooden table, Gus could see a big cake and lots of little pies and tarts cooling on a wire rack.

Licking his lips, Gus padded softly into the kitchen. He jumped up onto one of the kitchen chairs and put his paws on the table. He didn't know where to start! As well as the cake, there were custard tarts—another of Gus's favorites. And next to a big bowl of dough with a wooden spoon stuck in it, Gus spotted chocolate chip cookies!

But the big yellow cake with jam in the middle was nearest. Just as Gus opened his mouth to take a big bite out of it, Mrs. Wilson walked into the kitchen with Lulu in her arms.

"*Eeek!*" Mrs. Wilson screamed when she saw Gus. "Get away from my cake, you horrible little dog!"

"How dare you come into my house!" Lulu hissed at him, showing her sharp teeth.

Frightened, Gus jumped down and ran for the door. He rushed back

through the gap in the fence into the Mortons' yard, and through all the other yards, not stopping until he was safely back home.

"Gus, I've been looking for you!" Holly said as Gus trotted into the kitchen. "Where have you been?"

"I can guess," said Mrs. Carter. "On his usual round of visits to the neighbors!"

"Gus, have you been begging for food again?" Holly asked sternly.

Gus opened his eyes wide and tried to look as if he'd never dream of doing such a thing.

Holly couldn't help laughing. "You're a bad boy!" she said, stroking his soft coat.

"It's lucky our neighbors like him," Mrs. Carter remarked, "or they'd be complaining all the time!"

Right at that moment, Mrs. Wilson burst in through the kitchen door, making everyone, including Gus, jump. Her face was red and she looked very upset.

"Is something wrong, Mrs. Wilson?" Holly asked.

"Yes, something's very wrong!" Mrs. Wilson said angrily. "I want to complain about your dog. He ate my diamond ring!"

Chapter Two

"*What*?" gasped Holly and Mrs. Carter together.

Gus looked puzzled. He didn't even know what a diamond ring was. But whatever it was, he was sure he hadn't eaten it. He hadn't eaten anything in Mrs. Wilson's kitchen.

"He ate my diamond ring!" Mrs.

Wilson said again.

"Gus wouldn't eat a *ring*," Holly said.

"Why not?" Mrs. Wilson snapped. "That dog eats anything! Once he ate all the heads off my daffodils!"

"And they tasted *horrible!*" Gus barked indignantly.

"Gus, be quiet!" said Mrs. Carter.

Then she turned to Mrs. Wilson. "Why do you think Gus is to blame, Mrs. Wilson?"

"Because I found him climbing onto my kitchen table about five minutes ago!" Mrs. Wilson said angrily. "I'd taken my ring off and left it on the table while I was baking. When I came back, the ring was gone!"

Mrs. Wilson suddenly looked very sad. "The ring was a present from my husband," she said quietly. "It's very precious to me. I simply *must* get it back."

"I'm sorry, Mrs. Wilson," Holly said. "But I'm sure Gus didn't eat your ring."

Gus licked Holly's hand gratefully.

Mrs. Wilson shook her head. "He *must* have!" she declared.

"It *wasn't* me!" Gus howled. "Your stuck-up cat could have eaten the ring!"

"Be *quiet*, Gus!" Mrs. Carter said sharply.

Gus stopped howling. He hadn't seen Holly's mom get quite so angry before, and it scared him.

"I supposed Gus *might* have eaten the ring," Mrs. Carter said slowly. "He does like to eat very odd things sometimes."

"Oh, Mom!" Holly said. "Gus wouldn't eat a diamond ring. Not if there were cakes and cookies lying around."

"He would have gobbled down everything on the table if I hadn't walked in just then!" Mrs. Wilson said furiously. "That dog's a menace!"

Gus couldn't be quiet any longer, and he barked loudly. It wasn't fair! He hadn't eaten Mrs. Wilson's nasty old ring, and he didn't see why he should get the blame.

"Gus, be *quiet*!" shouted Mrs. Carter. "Holly, go and shut him in the living room while I talk to Mrs. Wilson."

"That dog needs to be taught some manners!" Mrs. Wilson sniffed.

"Sit down, Mrs. Wilson, and I'll make you a cup of tea," Holly's mom said. "Then we can talk about how we can find your ring."

Holly took Gus's collar and pulled

him out of the kitchen. Gus dug in his claws because he didn't want to leave. He wanted to stay there and tell Mrs. Wilson exactly what he thought of her. But in the end he gave in and let Holly take him into the living room.

"Oh, Gus," Holly sighed, kneeling down to put her arms around him. "I wish you hadn't gone into Mrs. Wilson's kitchen."

"So do I," Gus woofed miserably as he snuggled into her arms. "Then I wouldn't be in this mess!"

"If only you could talk!" Holly went on, looking just as miserable. "Then you could tell us what really happened."

Gus whined, and put his paw on

Holly's arm. He hated to see her so sad. And it was all his fault. That made him feel even worse.

"I'll go and see what Mom and Mrs. Wilson are saying," Holly told him. "Be a good boy, Gus, and don't make a noise."

She went out, closing the door behind her. Gus slumped down on the rug and put his nose between his paws. He felt very sad. If only he hadn't been so greedy, none of this would have happened. Now he had made Holly unhappy—and he'd made Mrs. Carter very angry.

Suddenly Gus sat up, feeling frightened. What if Mrs. Carter was *so* angry with him that he was sent back to the pound? Gus had been born at the pound and had lived there until the Carters had come looking for a puppy and had chosen him. That was the happiest day of Gus's life.

The pound was big and noisy and crowded. The people there were very busy. They didn't have time to play with him like Holly did. Gus didn't want to go back there. Besides, he loved Holly more than anyone else in the whole world, and he didn't want to leave her. So there was only one thing to do. . . .

Gus jumped up. He must find Mrs. Wilson's diamond ring himself, and show everyone that he hadn't eaten it!

Chapter Three

Gus looked around the living room, wondering how he could get out. The door was closed, but one of the windows was open just a little. Gus knew he wasn't allowed on the furniture, but this was an emergency. He leaped onto the big armchair near the window and scrambled up onto the windowsill.

Gus nudged the window open a little wider with his nose and looked out. It seemed an awfully long way down, and he felt nervous about jumping. But then Gus remembered Holly's sad face. He took a deep breath, jumped . . .

. . . and landed safely in the soft earth of the flower bed beneath the window.

"Yes!" he barked proudly. "I did it!"

Gus picked himself up and trotted through the yard. There was no time to waste. He had to get to Mrs. Wilson's house and find the ring before something awful happened to him.

"Hey, Gus!" Jock was in the Burtons' backyard, chewing on a large, juicy bone. He looked up as Gus raced past. "Do you want a lick? There's plenty here for two!"

Gus shook his head. "I'm not hungry!" he called, and he didn't slow down. He didn't care if he never saw a bone again, as long as he didn't have to leave Holly and go back to the pound.

Jock was so surprised, he dropped the bone. It rolled into the Burtons' fish pond, and Jock didn't even notice. "Gus isn't hungry?" he barked. "I don't believe it!"

When Gus reached the gap in the fence leading to Mrs. Wilson's backyard, he skidded to a halt, panting hard. Then he squeezed through the gap and trotted up the path to the kitchen door, looking carefully around him in case Mrs. Wilson was already on her way back home.

But this time the kitchen door was closed. Gus's heart sank. He should have guessed that Mrs. Wilson would lock her house before she left. But he had to find a way in. He had to.

Keeping a nervous lookout for Lulu, Gus went to investigate the back of the house. Gus wasn't the only dog on the street who was scared of Lulu. He'd seen the hefty white cat take on dogs before. She sent them running home with their tails between their legs as soon as she lashed out with her razor-sharp claws. But luckily Lulu was nowhere to be seen.

All the windows at the back of the house were closed. Gus ran up and down trying to find a way in, but there was not even a tiny gap he could squeeze through.

Gloomily, Gus went back to the kitchen door. What was he going to do? Somehow he had to get into that house, or he might be back in the pound before he could say *"Woof."* And then he'd never see Holly again. . . .

Gus whined and stood up on his back legs, putting his front paws on the kitchen door. He pushed at it as hard as he could, but it didn't move. It was then that Gus noticed a small opening at the bottom of the door. Lulu's cat door!

Gus was so excited that he had to stop himself from barking out loud. Eagerly he pushed his nose against the little door. It moved, and Gus stuck his head through into Mrs. Wilson's kitchen. Now for the rest of him. . . .

Carefully, Gus began to make his way through the hole in the door. He wriggled and he pushed and he just about got his front paws and shoulders inside. It was a very tight fit.

Gus tried to get his other half through the cat door. He wriggled and he pulled, but he couldn't move. He tried again and again, but his tummy was too big to get through the hole. He was stuck!

Gus began to feel very frightened. He didn't know what to do. He couldn't get in and he couldn't get out.

Then behind him he heard a silky voice say, "And what do you think you're doing in *my* cat door?"

Chapter Four

It was Lulu! Gus began to tremble with fear.

"You look very silly, indeed," Lulu said. Gus could almost hear her sharpening her claws gleefully. "I think you'd better come out, right now."

"I can't!" Gus whined miserably. "I'm stuck!"

"Serves you right for eating the diamond ring!" Lulu sniffed.

"I *didn't* eat it!" Gus said indignantly. "I've come to look for it. And—and I've got to find it because if I don't, I might get sent back to the pound and then I'll never see Holly again. . . ."

Lulu didn't say anything, and Gus began to feel even more nervous. He couldn't see what the cat was doing behind him, but he didn't want to stay and find out. He began to wriggle around again, trying to get through the cat flap into Mrs. Wilson's kitchen.

"Keep still!" Lulu hissed at him. "You'll never get in that way—you're too fat! You'd better try to come out again."

Gus knew that Lulu was right. He was just too big to get through the cat door. "But I can't get out again, either!" he wailed.

"Yes, you can!" Lulu said crossly. "You got in, didn't you? Just take it slowly."

Gus began trying to ease himself gently backward. At first he didn't move at all. He pulled harder . . . and harder. . . . Then, all of a sudden, he shot backward out of the cat door, like a cork out of a bottle, and tumbled head over heels onto the path.

"Thank you!" he woofed.

Lulu, who was washing herself, gave him a bored look. "Dogs!" she yawned.

"They're so stupid! I can show you a much better way to get into the house."

Gus stared at the cat in amazement.

"You want to get into the house, don't you?" Lulu jumped onto a trash can that stood underneath the kitchen windows. She began pulling at the smallest window with her claws, and after a minute or two, it swung open.

"The lock is broken," explained Lulu as she leaped down onto the path again. "If you can get up there, you can climb into the kitchen quite easily."

Gus could hardly believe his ears. Lulu, the cat who hated dogs, was helping him?

"Thank you!" he said. "But—but why are you helping me like this?"

"I came from the pound," Lulu said quietly. "I wouldn't want to go back there, either!"

The trash can was quite tall, but there was a big black bag of garbage lying next to it. Gus climbed onto the bag first and then managed to get onto the trash can. From there, it was easy for him to jump up onto the windowsill.

He peered through the window into Mrs. Wilson's kitchen. Just below him were the sink and draining board, which were piled with clean plates and cups.

Gus hopped down carefully onto the edge of the sink, but felt his front paw skidding on the slippery surface. *CRASH!*

As Gus knocked against the pile of china, plates and cups flew everywhere and smashed to bits as they hit the floor.

"I think that's called a crash landing," Lulu remarked as she came in through the cat door.

"Oh, no!" Gus muttered. "How did *that* happen?" He inspected his paw. He'd landed on a drop of dishwashing soap. No wonder he'd slipped!

He jumped down off the draining board. It wasn't a very good start. Still, he was sure Mrs. Wilson would forgive him if he found her diamond ring.

"Where are you going to start looking?" Lulu asked.

"I . . . um . . . don't know." Gus

suddenly realized that he didn't even know what a diamond ring was.

Lulu sighed. "You do *know* what a diamond ring is, don't you?"

"No," said Gus sadly.

Lulu told him. Gus couldn't help feeling alarmed when he found out how small it was. He looked around the enormous kitchen. How would he find a tiny little thing like a diamond ring in here? But he had to try, for Holly's sake.

First Gus went over to the kitchen table. He remembered that Mrs. Wilson said she'd left her ring there when she'd started cooking. All the tarts and cookies and the big bowl of dough were still there, but Gus wasn't interested in food.

He jumped up onto a chair and nosed around, looking for the ring.

CRASH! Lulu jumped as Gus accidentally knocked the plate of chocolate chip cookies onto the floor.

"Be careful!" she hissed.

Gus didn't care. He had to find that ring. But there was no sign of it on the kitchen table.

Next Gus sniffed his way all around the kitchen floor, in case the ring had fallen off the table. It hadn't.

Then he looked in all the cabinets he could reach. It wasn't easy, because it took him a long time to get each one open. The cabinets were so full of cans, bottles, and boxes of food that things kept falling out onto the floor.

Meanwhile, Lulu looked in all the places Gus couldn't reach, like the top of the refrigerator and the high shelves on the wall. But they didn't find the ring.

"It's not here!" Gus slumped down miserably on the kitchen floor. "What am I going to do?"

"We'd better get out of here," Lulu said, looking around the kitchen, "or we're going to be in big trouble."

Gus looked around the kitchen, too, and his heart sank. It was a mess. The floor was covered with pieces of broken china and cookies, along with cans and boxes of food. What on earth would Mrs. Wilson say when she saw it?

Lulu was right. They had to get out of there, and fast—before Mrs. Wilson came back.

Then Gus's ears pricked up. He could hear Holly's voice! He listened harder. Now he could hear Mrs. Carter and Mrs. Wilson talking. The voices were coming closer and closer. Gus could hear foot-steps, too.

Mrs. Wilson, Holly, and her mom were walking up the path to Mrs. Wilson's kitchen door!

Gus panicked. He ran over to the sink, but the draining board was too high for him to jump onto.

"Hide!" Lulu hissed, her tail swinging wildly from side to side.

Gus looked frantically around for somewhere to hide, but it was too late. The voices were already outside the back door!

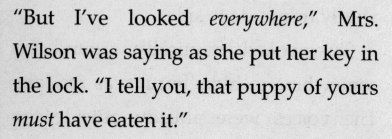

Chapter Five

"But I've looked *everywhere*," Mrs. Wilson was saying as she put her key in the lock. "I tell you, that puppy of yours *must* have eaten it."

"Gus can be a little naughty at times, Mrs. Wilson," Holly admitted, "but I'm *sure* he wouldn't have eaten your ring."

"Let's take another look for it," Mrs.

Carter added. "Holly and I will help you."

"It won't do any good," Mrs. Wilson sniffed, sounding rather tearful as she pushed open the kitchen door. "I know exactly where my ring is—inside your dog's tummy! I'm never going to get it back—" She swung the door open.

"Oh, no!" Mrs. Wilson stopped dead in the doorway. "Look at my kitchen!" she wailed.

"Well, everyone makes a little mess when they're baking," said Mrs. Carter, trying not to look shocked.

"I didn't do this!" Mrs. Wilson cried. "Oh! And look at my good china!" she shouted, as she noticed the mess by the sink.

Then she spotted Gus, who was trying to hide under the kitchen table. "Aha! I might have known!" Her face red with fury, Mrs. Wilson bent down under the table, grabbed Gus's collar, and pulled him out.

"Gus!" Holly gasped. "How on earth did you get in here?"

Gus whined. He was in real trouble now.

"Never mind how he got in here!" Mrs. Wilston retorted, still keeping a tight hold on Gus's collar. "Somehow he did, and just *look* at the mess he's made. *And* he's scared my cat!"

Lulu, who was sitting on top of the fridge watching what was going on, meowed loudly. "He didn't scare *me*!" she said, offended that anyone could think she found a mere puppy scary.

"I'm so sorry, Mrs. Wilson," said Holly's mom quickly. "I just don't understand how Gus got in. We'll pay for the damage, of course."

"Maybe he came to look for the ring," Holly said.

"Oh, very funny!" snorted Mrs. Wilson rudely.

"Don't be silly, Holly," said her mom.

"I'm not!" Holly insisted. "Maybe Gus was just trying to help."

Gus gave a yelp. At least Holly believed in him. He tried to pull away from Mrs. Wilson so that he could rush over to Holly and give her another grateful lick, but Mrs. Wilson was holding his collar too tightly. In fact, she was holding it so tightly it was beginning to hurt. Gus pulled harder, trying to get away.

"Now, I want to know what you're going to do about . . . this animal!" Mrs. Wilson demanded. "He's eaten my precious ring and messed up my kitchen, and I've just about had enough!"

Gus made one last effort to get away from Mrs. Wilson. Dragging her with him, Gus lunged forward toward Holly.

"Aah!" Mrs. Wilson screamed again as she fell against the table. The bowl of cookie dough toppled off and hit the floor with a loud noise. Big splats of sticky cookie dough flew everywhere, especially over Gus and Mrs. Wilson.

"Look what's he done!" Mrs. Wilson spluttered furiously as she tried to wipe the dough off her face. "That dog should be locked up—he's dangerous!"

"Oh, Gus!" Holly sighed. "What have you done *now*?"

But Gus wasn't listening. He could see something glittering in the cookie dough on the floor.

Chapter Six

"I want that dog out of my kitchen *now*!" Mrs. Wilson shouted angrily.

"Come on, Gus." Holly hurried across the kitchen toward him. "I think we'd better go.

Gus took no notice. He pushed his nose into the pile of cookie dough and barked loudly.

Holly knelt down beside him. "What are you doing, Gus?" she asked.

Gus barked again and scrabbled in the cookie dough with his paws.

Then Holly suddenly saw what he was trying to show her. "It's the ring!" she shouted, picking it up. "Gus has found the ring!"

"*What?*" Mrs. Wilson's eyes almost popped out of her head. "Let me see that!"

She grabbed the sticky, dough-covered ring, rushed over to the sink, and rinsed it clean. "It *is* my ring! Oh, thank goodness," she said in a shaky voice. "I thought it was gone forever!"

"It must have fallen into the bowl of

cookie dough!" said Mrs. Carter.

"It's a good thing you didn't make the rest of those cookies, Mrs. Wilson," said Holly. "The ring would have been inside, and someone *really* might have eaten it!"

Mrs. Wilson turned pale at the very thought and had to sit down on one of the kitchen chairs.

"Good job, Gus!" Holly said proudly, giving her puppy a big hug. "We never would have found the ring if it hadn't been for you!"

Gus began to bark joyfully. Thank goodness he'd managed to get himself out of trouble. But it had been a close call!

Mrs. Wilson looked around at the mess in her kitchen and frowned. "It was really very naughty of you to come into my kitchen, Gus," she said.

Gus hung his head. If he hadn't been so greedy in the first place, none of this would have happened.

Then Mrs. Wilson smiled. "But it was very clever of you to find my ring!" She slipped the ring onto her finger, then bent down and patted Gus on the head.

Gus licked her hand. Maybe now he and Mrs. Wilson could be friends.

"We'll help you clean up the kitchen, Mrs. Wilson," said Holly.

Mrs. Wilson looked pleased. "Thank you, Holly," she said.

Holly and her mom helped to tidy up. Then, carrying the big wedges of layer cake Mrs. Wilson had cut and wrapped for them, along with a pile of chocolate chip cookies, they said goodbye.

"From now on, there will always be a little something for you here when you're looking for a snack, Gus," Mrs. Wilson said. "It's the least I can do!"

"Yippee!" Gus barked happily.

"Just don't get any ideas about eating

my cat food," Lulu purred quietly from the top of the fridge.

When they got back home, Mrs. Carter went straight over to the refrigerator and took out a big, juicy bone. "I think Gus deserves a reward for finding Mrs. Wilson's ring!" she said with a smile.

"So do I!" said Holly. She took the bone and held it out to Gus. "Here you are, Gus! Good boy!"

Holly and her mom couldn't believe their eyes when Gus ignored the bone. Instead he flung himself at Holly, licking her hand and wagging his tail.

"Oh, Gus!" Holly laughed, dropping the bone and scooping her puppy into her arms. "Aren't you hungry?"

"Of course he's hungry!" Mrs. Carter laughed. "Gus is always hungry!"

But for once, Gus didn't care about the big, juicy bone. He was just glad to be back home safely, with Holly.

If he hadn't found Mrs. Wilson's ring, he might have been on his way back to the pound right now . . .

. . . *And if I hadn't been so greedy in the first place, I wouldn't have gotten into so much trouble*, Gus thought. *I'm not going to be so greedy ANYMORE!*

"I really don't think Gus wants this bone, Mom," said Holly.

Mrs. Carter looked surprised.

"Oh well, put it back in the fridge, and

he can have it later," she said. "Maybe Gus has decided to change his ways!"

"I have!" Gus yapped happily as Holly scooped him up and cuddled him. "I still love food, but not as much as I love you, Holly!"

He gave her a lick, then looked at her hopefully. "But when my appetite comes back," he woofed, "I'd be more than happy to help out with that cake!"

Puppy Friends Activity Fun Pages

 Developed by Stasia Ward Kehoe

Greedy Gus Trivia Quiz

1. What is Gus's favorite potato chip flavor?
2. Into what room does Holly shut Gus while her mother talks to Mrs. Wilson?
3. What was the happiest day of Gus's life?
4. Why does Lulu, the cat, decide to help Gus?
5. What is Gus's reward for finding Mrs. Wilson's ring?

(see answers at bottom of page)

Hidden Treasure Hunt

Gus had to look hard to find Mrs. Wilson's missing ring. Sometimes hunting for things can be fun! Host a treasure hunt in your backyard, basement, or playroom. Hide objects, such as small toys, costume jewelry, or plastic Easter eggs, in your treasure hunt area. On a large piece of paper, list everything you have hidden and hang the list in an easy-to-see place. Invite your friends to come and hunt for the treasures!

Answers: 1. Barbeque 2. The living room 3. The day Holly's family brought him home from the dog pound. 4. Because she also came from a pound and would not want to go back. 5. A juicy bone

Dog Breed Mix-Up

Everyone has a favorite breed of dog, be it the dashing dalmatian or the marvelous mutt. Try unscrambling the breed names below. Is your favorite listed? If not, make up your own dog breed word scramble—including your favorite breeds—and see if a family member or friend can unscramble it!

1. GLEEBA
2. OBREX
3. CREKOC EASIPNL
4. CHUDDSHNA
5. NEGOLD TIVEEERRR

6. ARGET ENAD
7. DERHUGONY
8. SHIIR RESTET
9. DOPOEL
10. SHLEW RETERIR

(see answers at bottom of page)

Puppy Pretzels

Gus loved Mrs. Wilson's baked treats. Try baking one of your own with some very doggy details—*be sure to ask an adult to help you in the kitchen.*

Ingredients:

1 tablespoon active dry yeast

2 teaspoons sugar

1 scant teaspoon salt

1 1/2 cups lukewarm water (105–115°F)

Answers: 1. Beagle 2. Boxer 3. Cocker Spaniel 4. Dachshund 5. Golden Retriever 6. Great Dane 7. Greyhound 8. Irish Setter 9. Poodle 10. Welsh Terrier

4 cups flour

1 egg

Coarsely ground salt, colored sugar sprinkles, or poppy or sesame seeds (optional)

Equipment: Mixing bowls, mixing spoons, measuring cup, measuring spoons, plastic wrap, baking sheet, pastry brush.

Put yeast, sugar and salt into a large mixing bowl. Stir in water. Gradually add flour, mixing until a soft dough forms. Knead the dough for about two minutes, then shape into a ball. Cover bowl with plastic wrap and allow dough to rise in a warm place for about one hour, or until doubled in size. Gently punch down dough to release air bubbles. Break off a golf-ball-sized piece of dough and roll it into a long rope, or "snake." Shape the rope into a dog face, bone, or pup with a wagging tail. Use little balls of dough to create eyes, ears, or other details. Place completed shape on lightly floured baking sheet. Continue making puppy pretzels until all dough has been used. Beat the egg with 1/2 teaspoon water until it is a smooth, yellow color. Gently brush the egg mixture over the pretzels. Sprinkle with salt, seeds, or sprinkles. Bake at 400°F for 25–30 minutes. Cool slightly and enjoy!

*Be sure to have some dog treats on hand to share with your pup while you're eating pretzels.

Puppy Care Pointer

"Rules of Chewing"

Puppies love—and need—to chew to help their adult teeth develop properly. However, growing dogs need to learn what they can and cannot chew, and that they should never use their teeth on humans. Be sure to have plenty of proper chewing toys to offer your puppy—especially when he tries to gnaw the leg of mom's chair or your favorite sneakers. There are a variety of methods for training a family dog to chew on food and toys instead of people and furniture. Consult a dog-raising manual, obedience specialist, or veterinarian to choose a method that is right for your pup.